FLY AWAY HOME

GENERAL EDITOR

JACK BOOTH

DAVID BOOTH

WILLA PAULI & JO PHENIX

IMPRESSIONS

HOLT, RINEHART AND WINSTON OF CANADA, LIMITED

Sponsoring Editor: Sheba Meland
Senior Editor: Wendy Cochran
Production Editor: Jocelyn Van Huyse
Art Director: Wycliffe Smith
Design Assistant: Julia Naimska
Cover Illustrator: Heather Cooper

ISBN 0-03-921406-0

Canadian Cataloguing in Publication Data

Main entry under title:
Fly Away Home

(Impressions)
For use in schools.
ISBN 0-03-921406-0

1. Readers (Primary). 2. Readers – 1950 –
I. Booth, Jack II. Series.

PE1119.H65   428.6   C83-098249-3

Illustrations
Maurice Sendak: pp. 4-12, 108-109; *Frank Hammond*: pp. 13, 82-89; *Dorothy Schmiderer*: pp. 14-18; *Frank Asch*: pp. 19-26; *Joanne Fitzgerald*: pp. 27, 28-29, 30-31, 52, 80-89; *Vladyana Krykorka*: p. 32; *Gail Geltner*: pp. 33-41; *Greg Duffell and Mary Young*: pp. 42-49; *Lisa Smith*: pp. 50-51; *San Murata*: pp. 53-59; *Joe Weissmann*: pp. 60-61; *Vesna Krysanovich*: p. 62; *Sami Soumalainen*: pp. 63-70; *Ron Berg*: pp. 71-76, 106-107; *Ken Stampnick*: pp. 77-79; *Sarie Jenkins*: pp. 97-105, 110-112; *Bill Harrison*: pp. 90-96.

The authors and publishers gratefully acknowledge the consultants listed below for their contribution to the development of this program:

Isobel Bryan   *Primary Consultant   Ottawa Board of Education*
Ethel Buchanan   *Language Arts Consultant   Winnipeg, Manitoba*
Heather Hayes   *Elementary Curriculum Consultant   City of Halifax Board of Education*
Gary Heck   *Curriculum Co-ordinator, Humanities   Lethbridge School District No. 51*
Ina Mary Rutherford   *Supervisor of Reading and Primary Instruction   Bruce County Board of Education*
Janice M. Sarkissian   *Supervisor of Instruction (Primary and Pre-School)   Greater Victoria School District*
Lynn Taylor   *Language Arts Consultant   Saskatoon Catholic School Board*

Acknowledgements
Mother Bear's Robin: Illustrations by Maurice Sendak and adapted text of "Mother Bear's Robin" from LITTLE BEAR'S VISIT by Else Holmelund Minarik. Copyright© 1961 by Else Holmelund Minarik. Pictures Copyright© 1961 by Maurice Sendak. An I CAN READ book. By permission of Harper & Row, Publishers, Inc. *Mix a Pancake*: By Christina Rossetti. From TIME'S DELIGHT chosen by Raymond Wilson, published by Beaver Books. *Alphabeast*: From THE ALPHABEAST BOOK by Dorothy Schmiderer. Copyright© 1971 by Dorothy Schmiderer. Reprinted by permission of Holt, Rinehart and Winston, Publishers. *Beans, Beans, Beans*: Reprinted from HOORAY FOR CHOCOLATE by Lucia & James L. Hymes, Jr. Copyright© 1960 by Lucia M. and James L. Hymes, Jr. A Young Scott book. By permission of Addison-Wesley Publishing Company, Reading, MA. *The Baby Beebee Bird*: An adaptation of the complete text of THE BABY BEEBEE BIRD by Diane Redfield Massie. Copyright © 1963 by Diane Redfield Massie. By permission of Harper & Row, Publishers, Inc. *Trouble in the Ark*: From TROUBLE IN THE ARK by Gerald Rose. Reprinted by permission of John Denton, Merlin Press, England. *This Tooth*: From ME by Lee Bennett Hopkins. Reprinted by permission of Curtis Brown Ltd. Copyright © 1970 by Lee Bennett Hopkins. *Henny Penny*: From the book HENNY PENNY by Paul Galdone, published by Clarion Books, Ticknor & Fields: A Houghton Mifflin Company, New York. Copyright © 1968 by the author. *Five Enormous Dinosaurs*: By permission of Oak Tree Publications, Inc. Copyright © 1978 by Dr. Fitzhugh Dodson. From I WISH I HAD A COMPUTER THAT MAKES WAFFLES. . . by Dr. Fitzhugh Dodson. All rights reserved. *Go Away, Dog*: The complete text of GO AWAY, DOG by Joan L. Nodset. Text copyright © 1963 by Joan L. Nodset. By permission of Harper & Row, Publishers, Inc.: New York. *The Coconut Game*: From INSIDE AND OUT in PATHFINDER — Allyn and Bacon Reading Program by Robert B. Ruddell et al. Copyright © 1978 by Allyn and Bacon, Inc. Used by permission. *Over There*: From HALLOWEENA HECATEE by Cynthia Mitchell. Reprinted by permission of William Heinemann Ltd. *Sean's Red Bike*: SEAN'S RED BIKE by Petronella Breinburg is published by The Bodley Head. *Pete's Puddle*: Copyright © 1950 by Joanna Foster, is reprinted by permission of Harcourt Brace Jovanovich, Inc. *I'll Be You, You Be Me*: Excerpt from I'LL BE YOU AND YOU BE ME, written by Ruth Krauss, illustrated by Maurice Sendak. Text copyright, 1954, by Ruth Krauss. Pictures copyright, 1954, by Maurice Sendak. By permission of Harper & Row, Publishers, Inc. *Song of the Train*: From FAR AND FEW by David McCord. Copyright © 1952 by David McCord. By permission of Little, Brown and Company.

Care has been taken to trace the ownership of copyright material used in this text. The publishers will welcome any information enabling them to rectify any reference or credit in subsequent editions.

Printed in Canada   4 5   87 86 85

Table of Contents

Mother Bear's Robin

by
Else Holmelund Minarik and Maurice Sendak

One spring day,
when Mother Bear was little,
she found a baby robin in the garden.
A baby robin, too little to fly.

"Oh, how sweet you are," she said.
"Where did you come from?"

"From my nest," said the robin.

"And where is your nest,
little robin?" asked Mother Bear.

"I think it is up there,"
said the robin.

No, that was a bluebird's nest.

"Maybe it is over there,"
said the robin.

No, that was an oriole's nest.

Mother Bear looked all over,
but could not find a robin's nest.

"You can live with me," she said.
"You can be my robin."

She took the robin in the house,
and made a little home for it.

"Please put me by the window,"
said the robin.
"I like to look out at the trees
and the sky."

Mother Bear put it by the window.

"Oh," said the robin,
"it must be fun to fly out there."

"It will be fun to fly in here,
too," said Mother Bear.

The robin ate. It grew. It sang.
Soon it could fly.
It flew about the house.
And that was fun,
just as Mother Bear had said.

But then, one day, it was unhappy.

Mother Bear asked,
"Why are you so sad, little robin?"

"I don't know," said the robin.
"My heart is sad."

"Sing a song," said Mother Bear.

"I cannot," said the robin.

"Fly about the house,"
said Mother Bear.

"I cannot," said the robin.

Mother Bear's eyes filled with tears.
She took the robin out
into the garden.

"I love you, little robin," she said.
"But I want you to be happy.
Fly away, if you wish.
You are free."

The robin flew, far up
into the blue sky.

It sang a high, sweet song.

Then down it came again,
right down to Mother Bear.

"Do not be sad," said the robin.
"I love you, too.
I must fly out into the world,
but I will come back.
Every year I will come back."

So Mother Bear kissed the robin,
and it flew away.
It came back.
And its children came back.
And its children's children too.

Mix a Pancake

by
Christina G. Rossetti

Mix a pancake,
Stir a pancake,
Pop it in the pan;

Fry the pancake,
Toss the pancake,
Catch it if you can.

Alphabeast
by
Dorothy Schmiderer

Aa

anteater

Ee

elephant

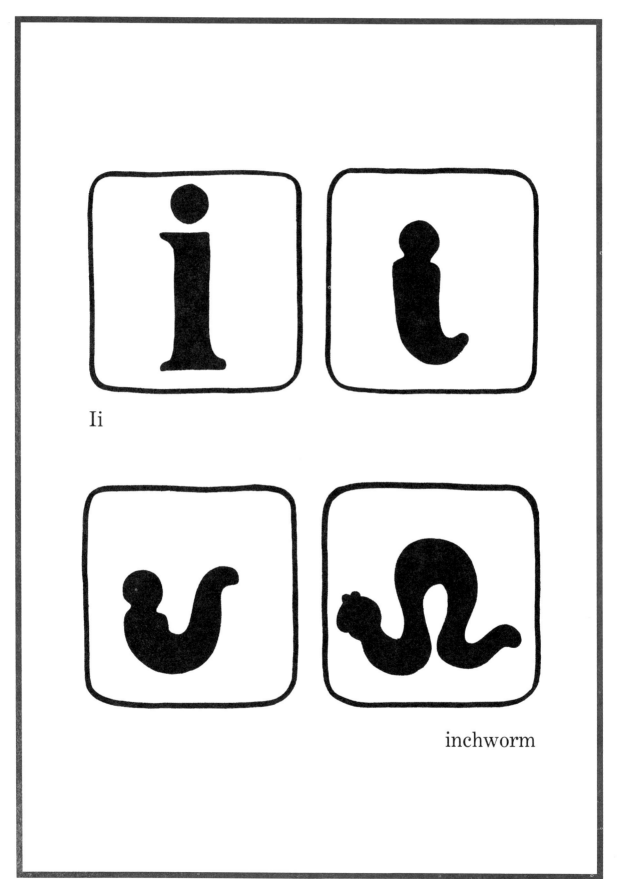

Ii

inchworm

Oo

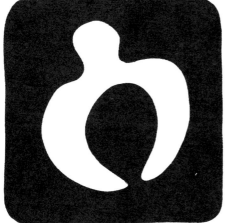

octopus

Uu

unicorn

The Last Puppy

by
Frank Asch

I was the last of Momma's nine puppies.

The last to eat from Momma,

the last to open my eyes,

the last to learn to drink milk from a saucer,

and the last one into the doghouse at night.

I was the last puppy.

One day Momma's owner put up a sign:
PUPPIES FOR SALE.

The next day, a little girl came
and took one of us away.

That night I couldn't sleep very well.

I kept wondering:
When will my turn come?
Will I be the last puppy again?

In the morning, a little boy came
to choose a puppy.

"Take me! Take me!" I barked.

"That puppy's too noisy," he said,
and picked another puppy instead.

Later that day, a nice lady
from the city almost picked me.

But when I tried to jump
into her lap, she fell backwards,
right into our bowl of milk.

When a farmer and his family came
to choose a puppy,
I got so excited
when the farmer picked me up,
I bit him on the nose.

They picked two puppies,
leaving four of us behind.

Soon there were just three of us left.

Then two.

Then just me, the last puppy.

But one day, my turn came, too.

Big hands picked me up
and gave me to a little boy.

We got into a car and drove away.

The little boy held me on his lap.

He put his face down close to mine
and I licked him on the nose.

He laughed and said,
"You know what?
You're my first puppy."

Beans, Beans, Beans

by
James L. Hymes Jr. and Lucia Hymes

Baked beans,
Butter beans,
Big fat lima beans,
Long thin string beans —
Those are just a few.

Green beans,
Black beans,
Big fat kidney beans,
Red hot chili beans,
Jumping beans too.

Pea beans,
Pinto beans,
Don't forget shelly beans.

Last of all, best of all,
I like jelly beans!

The Hamburger

by
Meguido Zola

Hamburger?
With everything?
Yes, but without...

mustard

relish

ketchup

bacon

mayonnaise

tomato

lettuce

onions

pickle

cheese.

One *plain* hamburger.

31

He Took a Fresh Egg

Traditional

He took a fresh egg and passed it to a friend,
Who took the fresh egg and passed it to a friend,
Who took the fresh egg and passed it to a friend,
Who took the fresh egg and passed it to a friend
Who dropped it.

The Baby Beebee Bird

by
Diane Massie

The animals at the zoo had roared
and growled all day long.
They were very tired.

"It's time to go to sleep,"

said the 🐘.

Soon the zoo was very still.

"Bee bee bobbi bobbi!
Bee bee bobbi bobbi!"
"What," said the , "is that?"
"It's the baby beebee  ,"
said the .
"He's new to the zoo."
"Well, tell him to be quiet,"
growled the  .
"I want to sleep."
"Bee bee bobbi bobbi!
Bee bee bobbi bobbi!"
"Be quiet, please," said the .
"But I can't,"
said the baby beebee  .

"I'm wide awake.
    Bee bee bobbi bobbi,
    bee bee bobbi bobbi."
"Quiet!" roared the 🦁.
    "He's wide awake," said the 🦒.
"Why isn't he tired like the rest
of us?" growled the 🐆.
    "Aren't you tired?"
asked the 🦒.

"No," said the baby beebee 🐦.
"I was sleeping all day long.
Now it's time for me to sing.
    Bee bee bobbi bobbi,
    bee bee bobbi bobbi!"

"Oh, dear," said the .
"I am so tired."

"Bee bee bobbi bobbi,
 bee bee bobbi bobbi,"
went the baby beebee 🐦.

"Quiet!" yelled all the animals.
"We can't sleep!"

"Bee bee bobbi bobbi,
bee bee bobbi bobbi,"
  went the baby beebee
  all night long.

In the morning the animals
were very tired.

"What has happened?"
said the keeper.

"The 🐭 is still asleep.

The 🦁 is standing on his head.

The 🐻 won't play.

Dear Me!"

"Bee bee bobbi bobbi,"
said the baby beebee 🐦
one more time.
Then he went to sleep.

The animals
talked quietly
to each other.
They looked at
the baby beebee 🐦 .
He was sleeping.

"Bee bee bobbi!" roared the 🦁 .
"Bee bee bobbi!" called the 🐘 .
"Bee bee bobbi!" growled the 🐆 .
"Bee bee bobbi bobbi!"
yelled all the animals together.
"Quiet," said the baby beebee 🐦 .

"I am trying to sleep."

"Bee bee bobbi bobbi!"
yelled the animals.

The keeper ran up.
"What is it now?" he said.
But no one could tell him.
All day long the animals yelled,
"Bee bee bobbi bobbi."

The baby beebee
could not sleep at all.

The  went down and
the came up.
"Bee bee bobbi bobbi," said the
very quietly.
He was too tired to roar.
"Bee bee bobbi bobbi,"
said the very quietly.
He was too tired to talk.
"Bee bee," said the .
He was too tired to say more.
And then all was still.

The 🌙 looked down
on a sleeping zoo.
Not a 🕷 moved.
Not an 🐱 moved.
Not a 🐍 moved.
And the baby beebee 🐦
was asleep high up in his tree.
Night is best for sleeping,
even for a very little beebee 🐦 .

Trouble in the Ark

by
Gerald Rose

All the animals were crowded in the ark.

It rained and rained and rained.

They became very fed up.

It was fly who started the trouble.

He *buzzed* mouse

who SQUEAKED at rabbit

who *squealed* at rhinoceros

who **snorted** at parrot

who SQUAWKED at snake

43

who *chattered* at pig

who **grunted** at duck

who QUACKED at dog

who BARKED at cow

who MOOED at bull

who BELLOWED at owl

who HOOTED at horse

who NEIGHED at goose

who HONKED at hedgehog

who SNUFFLED at wolf

who HOWLED at hen

who CACKLED at cat

who ScREECHED at lion

who ROARED at elephant

who TRUMPETED at Noah

who said:
"I can't stand
this noise any longer."

Just then dove flew in with an olive twig.

The rain stopped and Noah's wife sighted land.

Noah was delighted.

All the animals
were glad to leave
the ark and Noah
and his wife
were left in peace...

well, almost.

Tongue Trouble

Traditional

Swan, swim over the sea.
Swim, swan, swim!
Swan, swim back again.
Swim, swan, swim!

This Tooth
by
Lee Bennett Hopkins

I jiggled it
jaggled it
jerked it.

I pushed
and pulled
and poked it.

But—

As soon as I stopped, and left it alone,
This tooth came out on its very own.

Henny Penny
by
Paul Galdone

One day, Henny Penny was picking up corn
in the farmyard when—whack!
An acorn hit her on the head.

"Goodness gracious me!" said Henny Penny.
"The sky is falling! I must go and tell the King."

So she went along and she went along
and she went along, until she met Cocky Locky.

"Cock-a-doodle-doo! Where are you going,
Henny Penny?" asked Cocky Locky.

"Oh," said Henny Penny, "the sky is falling
and I am going to tell the King."

"May I go with you, Henny Penny?"
asked Cocky Locky.

"Yes, indeed," said Henny Penny.

So Henny Penny and Cocky Locky went off
to tell the King that the sky was falling.

They went along and they went along
and they went along, until they met Ducky Lucky.

"Quack, quack, quack! Where are you going,
Henny Penny and Cocky Locky?" asked Ducky Lucky.

"Oh, we are going to tell the King
that the sky is falling,"
said Henny Penny and Cocky Locky.

"May I go with you?" asked Ducky Lucky.

"Yes, indeed," said Henny Penny and Cocky Locky.

So Henny Penny, Cocky Locky, and Ducky Lucky
went off to tell the King that the sky was falling.

They went along and they went along
and they went along, until they met Goosey Loosey.

"Honk, honk, honk! Where are you going,
Henny Penny, Cocky Locky, and Ducky Lucky?"
asked Goosey Loosey.

"Oh, we are going to tell the King
that the sky is falling," said Henny Penny,
Cocky Locky, and Ducky Lucky.

"May I go with you?" asked Goosey Loosey.

"Yes, indeed," said Henny Penny, Cocky Locky, and Ducky Lucky.

So Henny Penny, Cocky Locky, Ducky Lucky, and Goosey Loosey went off to tell the King that the sky was falling.

They went along and they went along
and they went along, until they met Turkey Lurkey.

"Gobble, gobble, gobble!" said Turkey Lurkey.

"Where are you going, Henny Penny, Cocky Locky, Ducky Lucky, and Goosey Loosey?"

"Oh, we are going to tell the King
that the sky is falling," said Henny Penny,
Cocky Locky, Ducky Lucky, and Goosey Loosey.

"May I go with you?" asked Turkey Lurkey.

"Yes, indeed," said Henny Penny, Cocky Locky, Ducky Lucky, and Goosey Loosey.

So Henny Penny, Cocky Locky, Ducky Lucky, Goosey Loosey, and Turkey Lurkey went off to tell the King that the sky was falling.

They went along and they went along and they went along, until they met Foxy Loxy.

"Where are you going, Henny Penny, Cocky Locky, Ducky Lucky, Goosey Loosey, and Turkey Lurkey?" asked Foxy Loxy.

"Oh, we are going to tell the King that the sky is falling," said Henny Penny, Cocky Locky, Ducky Lucky, Goosey Loosey, and Turkey Lurkey.

"Ah, ha!" said Foxy Loxy.
"But this isn't the way to the King,
Henny Penny, Cocky Locky, Ducky Lucky,
Goosey Loosey, and Turkey Lurkey.
Come with me and I will show you
a shortcut to the King's palace."

"Oh, good!" said Henny Penny, Cocky Locky,
Ducky Lucky, Goosey Loosey, and Turkey Lurkey.

They went along and they went along
and they went along, until they reached
Foxy Loxy's cave.

In they all went after Foxy Loxy.

From that day to this,
Turkey Lurkey, Goosey Loosey,
Ducky Lucky, Cocky Locky,
and Henny Penny
have never been seen again.
And the King has never been told
the sky is falling.

Foxy Loxy and Mrs. Foxy Loxy
and their seven little foxes
still remember the fine feast they had that day.

Five Enormous Dinosaurs
by
Dr. Fitzhugh Dodson

Five enormous dinosaurs
  Letting out a roar;
One went away,
And then there were four.

  Four enormous dinosaurs
  Munching on a tree;
One went away,
  And then there were three.

Three enormous dinosaurs
Didn't know what to do;
One went away,
And then there were two.

  Two enormous dinosaurs
    Having lots of fun;
      One went away,
        And then there was one.

      One enormous dinosaur
      Afraid to be a hero;
He went away,
    And then
      there was—zero!

Go Away, Dog

by
Joan L. Nodset

Go away,
you bad old dog.
Go away from me.
I don't like you, dog.

I don't like dogs at all.
Big dogs, little dogs.
Any dogs at all.

I don't want that stick.
Don't give it to me.

S. SUOMALAINEN

Don't wag
your tail at me.
I don't like dogs.

You aren't bad for a dog.
But I don't like dogs.

Say, do that again.
Roll over again, dog.
Say, that's not bad.

Can you
shake hands?
This is how to shake hands.

I didn't say to lick my hand.
Stop that, you old dog.

If I play with you,
will you go away?

If I throw the stick,
will you go away?

There now, go away with your stick.

What do you want now?

If I throw it again,
will you go away?

Don't jump on me, dog.
I don't like that.

Go away, you old dog.
Go on home now.

Don't you have a home?
Well, that's too bad.
But you can't come home with me.

All right, let's run, dog.
Can you run as fast as I can?

You can run fast all right.

That was fun, dog.
Maybe we can play again.

But I have to go home now.
No, you can't come.
Go away now, dog.

Don't look so sad, dog.
Don't look that way at me.
Can I help it if you
don't have a home?

Why don't you go away?

You like me, don't you, you old dog?
Well, I like you, too.

All right, I give up.

Come on home, dog.
Come on, let's run.

The Coconut Game

by

Mark Taylor

One day Elephant fell into a pit.
"Help!" cried Elephant.
The animals ran and looked
into the pit.
"We can't help you, Elephant,"
they said.
"You are too big
and the pit is too deep."
The animals could not help Elephant.
One by one they went away

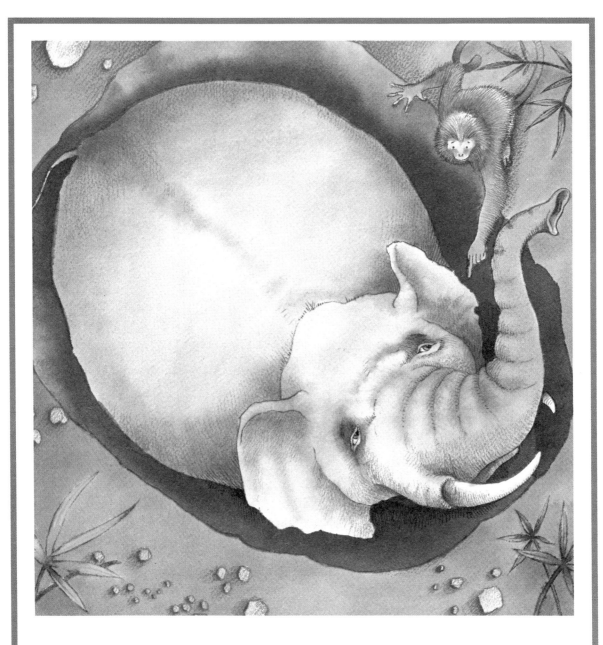

"Elephant!" called Monkey
from the top of the pit.
"I'll get you out."

"But how?" asked Elephant.
"You are so little."

"Not too little," said Monkey.
And away she ran.

Soon Monkey came back.
She had a ladder with her.
Elephant tried to climb up the ladder,
but when he got on it,
the ladder broke.
"It's no use," said Elephant.
"How will I get out of this pit?"

"You will see," said Monkey.
And away she ran.

Soon Monkey came back.
She had a rope with her.
Elephant took hold of the rope.
Then Monkey pulled on it.
But Monkey could not
pull Elephant out of the pit.
"It's no use," said Elephant.
"How will I get out of this pit?"

"You will see," said Monkey.
And away she ran.

Soon Monkey came back.
Many, many monkeys were with her.
Each monkey had a coconut.
"Let's play the Coconut Game,"
said Monkey.
Monkey began to roll a coconut
into the pit.

All the other monkeys began
to roll coconuts into the pit.
"Why are you rolling coconuts
into this pit?" cried Elephant.
Elephant was very angry.
He stomped on the coconuts.
He jumped up and down
on the coconuts.
Elephant grew more and more upset.
But still the monkeys rolled coconuts
into the pit.

All at once Elephant found himself
close to the top of the pit.
He walked right out of it!
All the monkeys laughed and jumped.
"Didn't you know that someone small
can help someone big?"
asked Monkey.

"No," said Elephant,
"but now I do!"

Over There

by
Cynthia Mitchell

Over the people,
Over the wall,
Over the top
of the chimneys tall,
Over the steeple,
Over the ridge,
Over the top
of the railway bridge.

Over the fountains,
Over the streams,
Over the tops
of the lighthouse beams,
Over the mountains,
Over the seas,
Over the tops
of the forest trees.

Over the rice fields,
Over the kites,
Over the top
of the Northern Lights,
Over the icefields,
Over the snow,
Right to the ends
of the earth we'll go.

An Ice Cream Wish

by
Melanie Zola

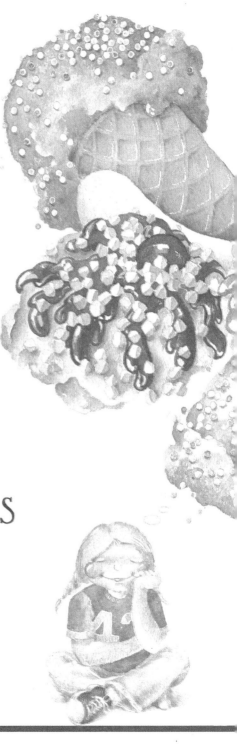

1 ice cream cake

2 ice cream sundaes

3 ice cream floats

4 ice cream logs

5 ice cream balls

6 ice cream sandwiches

7 ice cream cones

8 ice cream whirls

9 ice cream scoops

10 ice cream banana splits with vanilla,
chocolate, strawberry
cherries, nuts,
and me

Sean's Red Bike

by
Petronella Breinburg

The moment Sean saw the red bicycle
in the shop window, he wanted it.

"But that one costs
a lot of money," said Mum.
"How about a new three-wheeler?"

But Sean didn't want
a new three-wheeler.

"I want that red bike," he said,
"with a shiny new bell."

One day Sean helped
Patrick's dad to wash his car.

Sean worked very hard
washing and polishing,
and Patrick's dad paid him fifty cents.

"For your red bike," he said.

Another day Uncle Fred
came to visit the family.

He gave Sean fifty cents.
"For your red bike," he said.

So every week
Sean took his pocket money
to the shop.

"Not long now,
not long now,"
said the storekeeper.

For two days running,
Sean helped Aunt Hillary
to look after baby Jerome.

For each day Sean earned
fifty cents.

"For your red bike,"
said Aunt Hillary.

Then late
one afternoon,
the red bike
was delivered
to Sean's home.

"It's here, it's here!
My red bike is here!"
Sean yelled
from the window.

Everyone came out to see
Sean's new red bike.

"The bike's too big for you, Sean,"
said John.

"Bet you can't ride it,"
said the bigger boy
from next door.

"Bet I can," said Sean.

"Will you hold it at the back while I start?" he asked the big boy.

After only a few wobbly paces there was a crash and Sean was down on the road.

He struggled to his feet, trying not to cry.

Once again, Sean
got on his new bike,
and this time
he got as far as the corner
before he fell off.

"I'll go around the corner
tomorrow," said Sean.
"I had better go in now."

Then he proudly wheeled
his new red bike
in through
the front door.

The Ants Go Marching
by
Bernice Freschet

The ants come marching
one by one,
up and up,
out of the earth,
zigging and zagging
in a long line...

Where are they marching
one by one?
do they know? do they know?

Two by two
the ants come marching,
over a stick,
over a leaf,
over a foot,
a furry foot,
a big rabbit's foot.

Almost last
comes Little Ant.

HARRISON

Where are they marching
two by two?
Do they know? Do they know?

The ants come marching
three by three.
Little Ant stops
beside a rock.
Up he climbs,
and over and down.
A caterpillar crawls away.

Where are they marching
three by three?
Do they know? Do they know?

Four by four
the ants come marching,
up a hill, over a log
that crosses a brook.
Beneath the log
fish go swimming,
swimming by.

Where are they marching
four by four?
Do they know?
Do they know?

Five by five
the ants come marching,
through the tall grass,
the green grass,
the whispering grass.
Last of all
comes Little Ant.
Hurry, hurry, Little Ant!

Where are they marching
Five by five?
Do they know? Do they know?

Six by six
the ants come marching,
down the path,
not looking right,
not looking left,
not looking at the
bumpy toad....
Watch out, Little Ant!
Not too close
to the bumpy old toad!

Where are they marching
six by six?
Do they know?
Do they know?

The ants come marching
seven by seven,
up a daisy,
down again,
up a thistle
and down.
On, Little Ant!
On! Quickly!

Where are they marching
seven by seven?
Do they know?
Do they know?

Eight by eight
the ants come marching,
side by side,
all but Little Ant.
He's far behind.
Scurry,
Little Ant,
scurry....

Where are they marching
eight by eight?
Do they know?
Do they know?

The ants come marching
nine by nine,
under a fence,
under a horse,
under a cow,
across a meadow.

Where are they marching
nine by nine?
Do they know?
Do they know?

Look! Little Ant...look!
Wonderful food
is spread under a tree!

They march
ten by ten
to the picnic lunch....

What delicious food!
Enough,
enough for an army,
an army of ants,
and more than enough
for Little Ant.

Soon, off they march.
Side by side,
the ants go marching. . . .

Ten by ten

Nine by nine

Eight by eight

Seven by seven

Six by six

Five by five

Four by four

Three by three

Two by two

And last of all
comes Little Ant.

Where are they marching?
Hurrying, scurrying,
busy little ants.
Do they know?
Do they know?

Down...
they march.
Down
in the earth,
the quiet earth,
the warm earth,
the good earth.

They know,
they know.
They're marching
home.

Pete's Puddle

by
Joanna Foster

Splish! Splish! Splosh!

Today is a puddle day.
And Pete sees
puddles everywhere.

There are puddles
in the street.

Whish!

go the cars
through the puddles
in the street.

So Pete can't walk
in these puddles.

There are puddles
on the sidewalk.

Swish!

goes the broom
through the puddles
on the sidewalk.

So Pete can't play
in these puddles.

But there's a great big puddle
in the backyard,
a puddle just for Pete.

And...
in Pete's puddle
Pete goes

Splish!
Splash!
Splosh!

with his big red rubber boots.

Pete goes

Mish!
Mash!
Muddle!

with his hands
in the mud.

Pete plays it's a sea
and sails his red boat upon it.

Pete plays it's a mirror
and sees his face shining in it.

Pete plays he's a builder
and makes a dam across his puddle.

Pete plays he's a giant
and makes great footprints
in the mud.

Pete plays he's a cook
and makes mud pies
for his supper.

Pete plays he's a milkman
and fills bottles in his puddle.

Pete looks into his puddle
and sees a worm
come out of the ground.

Pete looks into his puddle
and sees the whole world
upside down.

Pete looks into his puddle
and sings this puddle song:

Puddle, Puddle, Puddle,
Splish! Splash! Splosh!
Puddle, Puddle, Puddle,
Mish! Mash! Muddle!
Puddle, Puddle, Puddle
Piddle, Paddle, Puddle,
On
A
Day
Like
This!

I'll Be You, You Be Me

by
Ruth Krauss and Maurice Sendak

He runs.

I run.

He jumps.

I jump.

He dunks his toast

and I dunk mine.

He calls, "Watch out, Lady!"

I call, "Watch out, Lady!"

He's practically my brother.

We take walks

and hold hands.

We trade things,

and if he didn't have a squirt-gun

and he wanted a squirt-gun

and I didn't have a squirt-gun,

I'd get one for him.

And when I go away,

he gives me a present

and ties it up special with ribbons,

and it is to keep.

Song of the Train

by
David McCord

Clickety-clack.
Wheels on the track.
This is the way
They begin the attack:

Clack-ety-clack.
Click-ety-clack.
Click-ety, clack-ety.
Click-ety
Clack.

Riding in front.
Riding in back.
Everyone hears
The song of the track:
Clickety-clack.
Clickety-clack.
Clickety, clickety.
Clackety
Clack.

Clickety-clack.
Over the crack.
Faster and faster
The song of the track:
Clickety-clack.
Clickety-clack.
Clickety-clack.
Clickety, clackety.
Clackety
Clack.